THE FACTS ABOUT

ALZHEIMER'S DISEASE

BY
Laurie Beckelman

CONSULTANT
Elaine Wynne, M.A., Licensed Psychologist

CRESTWOOD HOUSE
New York

LIBRARY OF CONGRESS CATALOGING IN PUBLICATION DATA

Beckelman, Laurie.
  The facts about Alzheimer's disease
  Summary: Explains the causes and effects of Alzheimer's, and discusses myths about the disease.

  p. cm.—(The Facts about)
  1. Alzheimer's disease—Juvenile literature. I. Title. II. Series.
RC523.B4   1990   618.97'6831—dc20   89-25251   CIP
ISBN 0-89686-489-8   AC

PHOTO CREDITS

Cover: Image Works
Devaney Stock Photos: 4, 14, 23, 38-39; (William R. Wright) 37
DRK Photo: (Dwight R. Kuhn) 10; (Stephen J. Krasemann) 24; (David Falconer) 31
Photo Researchers: (Jerry Wachter) 13; (Blair Seitz) 17; (David R. Frazier) 42-43
Image Works: (Mike Douglas) 18; (Bob Daemmrich) 32, 34
Journalism Services: (John Patsch) 27
Office of Technology Assessment: 28-29

CRESTWOOD HOUSE

Macmillan Publishing Company
866 Third Avenue
New York, NY 10022
Collier Macmillan Canada, Inc.

Printed in the United States of America
First Edition
10 9 8 7 6 5 4 3 2 1

TABLE OF CONTENTS

CAN YOU ANSWER THESE QUESTIONS?

Here's a quiz. See if you can answer these questions:
1. Who is the president of the United States?
2. What is today's date?
3. What is 3 + 2?

That's a snap, you're probably thinking. Anyone could answer those questions.

But at 74 years old, Ida Indik could not.

Ida Indik was my grandmother. She was not an educated woman, but she was bright. For years, she had managed the many details of running a home and raising a family. She spoke three languages. She could follow detailed patterns to knit scarves and vests. Yet, at 74, she could not remember the date.

My family knew this because a doctor asked my grandmother the date, as well as the other questions you just answered. He was trying to tell if she had a brain disease called *Alzheimer's disease*. She did. She was one among many.

Alzheimer's disease is the leading cause of *mental decline* in the aged. No one knows just how many older Americans have the disease. But experts agree that the number is large–2.5 to 3 million. Over time, this disease destroys its victims' minds. It robs them of the skills and memories, ideas and feelings, senses of humor and dreams that made them who they were.

Over time, Alzheimer's disease robs its victims of memories, skills, and ideas.

5

These men and women lose the ability to remember. To learn. To think. They may become secretive, angry, or afraid. They may forget the most basic social skills—when to use a fork or a napkin, for instance. Their disease may leave them unable to follow directions, to add, or to subtract. They may not recognize things, people, or words they once knew or remember how to bathe, dress, feed, or otherwise care for themselves.

They may die because of Alzheimer's disease. The disease that cripples their minds also weakens their bodies. Alzheimer's disease cuts patients' *life expectancy*. On average, someone with Alzheimer's disease will continue to live only half as many more years as a healthy person the same age.

The disease doesn't kill directly, but makes patients more likely to catch illnesses that will kill them. Many Alzheimer's patients die of *pneumonia*. Doctors recognize Alzheimer's disease as the real killer, however. Alzheimer's disease is now the fourth leading cause of death in this country. It ranks just behind such fatal illnesses as cancer, heart disease, and *stroke*.

Why haven't you heard more about it? For one thing, doctors used to think Alzheimer's was rare. As late as 1968, a pamphlet from the National Institute of Mental Health said:

> The two chief...brain-killers are *cerebral arterio-sclerosis* and senile brain disease....Two others, Alzheimer's Disease and Pick's Disease, usually strike a few years earlier, and are rarer.

Experts thought Alzheimer's was a disease that afflicted middle-aged people. This was because of the way the disease was discovered.

A DOCTOR'S DISCOVERY

In 1906, a German *neurologist* named Alois Alzheimer made an important discovery. Dr. Alzheimer studied the brain and brain diseases. One of his patients was a woman who had been losing her memory for five years. She had become less and less able to think clearly or to remember where she was. Sometimes she thought she was living in the past.

As her illness got worse, her sense of time and place failed more and more often. She was less able to control her emotions and behavior. She was suffering from *dementia.*

When this patient died, Dr. Alzheimer did an *autopsy.* He removed tissue from her brain and looked at it under a microscope.

What he saw was not normal. In many *nerve cells,* hairlike parts that should be straight were tangled. And in areas around nerve cells, Dr. Alzheimer saw large, dark spots. He called them *plaques.* Later, scientists learned that plaques are piles of dead cell parts.

Dr. Alzheimer wrote about the plaques and *tangles* and the mental and emotional changes he thought they caused. This was the first description of Alzheimer's disease.

Dr. Alzheimer's patient was only 56 years old when she died. We now know that this is unusually young for an Alzheimer's patient. But for many years, doctors didn't know that. They thought Alzheimer's was a disease of middle age. They even called it *presenile dementia*. That means a loss of mental skills that starts before age 65. Since they didn't see many middle-aged patients who were senile, they thought Alzheimer's disease was rare.

But they did see older people with memory loss and other Alzheimer's *symptoms*. For a long time, this *senile* (after 65) *dementia* was thought to be a normal part of aging. All old people, it was thought, would eventually become senile. Today, we know this isn't true. We know that changes in the way people's brains work are signs of disease.

DON'T ALL OLD PEOPLE BECOME SENILE?

The thought that all old people become senile is just one of several false ideas about old age and Alzheimer's disease. Another is that any older person who forgets things or acts "crazy" has Alzheimer's disease. This simply isn't true.

Some small amount of forgetting is a normal part of aging for many people. An older person may for a moment forget the name of a favorite tea. He or she may forget

some of the advice the doctor gave for treating a sprained wrist.

But Alzheimer's patients may not remember where they keep their tea. Or that they need to boil water to make it. They may not remember spraining a wrist at all and thus may blame someone else for the injury. They forget basic, familiar routines: the way to a son's house two blocks away; how to tie shoes; how to pay bills. This forgetting disrupts daily life. And it doesn't pass. In time, the healthy person usually remembers a forgotten name—or, if told again, will learn it. This is not so with Alzheimer's patients. They may have better days and worse, but slowly, over time, their memories fail more and more often. As the disease gets worse, their behavior and personalities also change.

Alzheimer's is not the only disease that can cause memory problems and odd behavior in the elderly, however. Doctors now know of more than 70 causes of such changes. Many of these are treatable. For instance, some medications cause Alzheimer's-like changes in some older people. By changing the patient's medicine, a doctor can eliminate the symptoms.

Depression can also cause memory loss and changes in behavior. It is often treatable with medication. Multiple small strokes are another cause of Alzheimer's-like symptoms. The damage—and dementia—caused by these strokes cannot be undone. Doctors can take steps to limit the likelihood of more strokes and more damage, however. The patient need not get worse.

Although Alzheimer's patients have good days and bad days, the disease slowly disrupts a person's routine.

Alzheimer's disease, however, is neither curable nor treatable yet. Today, no one can stop its progress. And it is the most common form of dementia in the elderly.

WHO IS AT RISK?

Ruth had always been careful about her health. Long before natural foods became the rage, she ate brown rice and tofu. She walked every day and tended her garden. "A good person," "always up," "friendly"–that's how people described her.

If you asked Ruth, she'd say her life was charmed. She was healthy. She had raised three loving children. Her husband was her best friend. What more could she want?

But shortly after Ruth turned 70, her husband found her staring at the stove, puzzled. She could not remember how to make her famous chili. She had, he realized, been forgetting a lot of things lately–even to water her beloved garden. Ruth was in the early stages of Alzheimer's disease.

Henry's life had been different. A cigar-smoking, hard-drinking film producer, he was always on the run. He often flew between New York, Los Angeles, and London. When he wasn't working, he was at a restaurant with friends, or at a fundraiser, or at a party. He rarely stopped to catch his breath. When he did, he had to admit that some of his running was running away–away from the memory of a son killed in a car crash.

That crash had almost killed Henry, too. Not when he lost control of the car, but after, when the guilt over his son Jonathan's death was too much. Henry had tried to end his own life. He had spent a month in a hospital and a longer time on medication to treat his depression.

When Henry got Alzheimer's disease, friends said maybe it was because of the stress of his son's death. Or maybe it was because he worked too hard. They were wrong.

So far, experts have found no habits or life events that make someone more or less likely to get the disease. Alzheimer's strikes people who eat fast foods and people who eat health foods. It strikes people who smoke and people who don't. It affects women and men, blacks and

All types of people can get Alzheimer's, even healthy people concerned about their exercise and eating habits.

whites. Some patients have had easy lives, others hard. Some have been healthy, others sickly. Some have had mental illnesses, others not. Nothing predicts who will get Alzheimer's disease.

One form of the disease that strikes middle-aged people is *inherited*, which means that parents may pass it on to their children. A person whose blood relative gets the disease at age 40 has a 40 percent chance of also getting the disease. But this form is rare. Someone whose relative gets Alzheimer's at age 80 is at no greater risk than anyone else.

One in four people eighty-five years and older can get Alzheimer's disease.

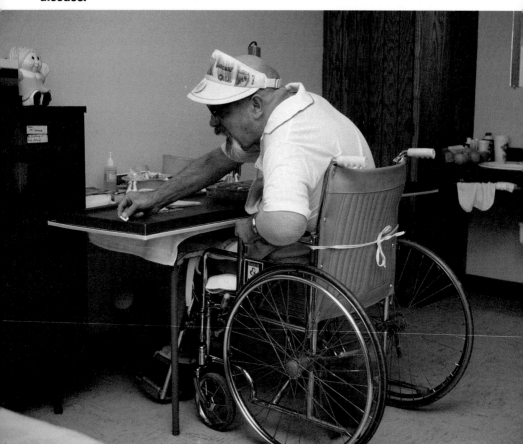

Age is the only clear factor in developing Alzheimer's disease. The older the person, the greater his or her chance of getting the disease. That chance is one in one hundred for someone aged sixty-five, says a government report. For someone aged eighty-five, however, it is one in four. Since more Americans are living longer now, more are getting Alzheimer's disease.

Of course, even a one-in-four risk means that most people never get Alzheimer's disease. Most older people – even the "old" old – can think, plan, reason, and even remember as well as young people. In fact, in some areas they do better. Studies show that memory of facts about the world may get better with age. And in a study of vocabulary, older adults did 18 percent better than young adults. All the people in this study had gone to the same college and so were fairly well matched for education.

Our world is filled with people who live rich, productive lives well into old age. Former president Ronald Reagan was 77 when he left office. Claude Pepper was still a congressman when he died at 88. The painter Georgia O'Keeffe lived and worked into her 90s. The writer Malcolm Cowley wrote an article for *The New York Times* called "Being Old Old." He was 87 when he wrote it.

These are all famous people. But many of us have our own models of vibrant old age. I grew up with three grandparents. One grandmother was still baking cakes at age 87. My grandfather died at 80, his car keys and an open book at his side. But my other grandmother had Alzheimer's disease. Why her? No one in her life can tell.

A GRANDMOTHER NAMED IDA

My Grandma Ida was a grandmother with a capital *G*. She was all warm smiles and softness. She wore her hair long, in an old-fashioned braid wrapped like a crown around her head. I sometimes thought the braid was silly. But when Grandma cut it off to "join the modern world," I felt sad. And I was glad she didn't do anything else to change–like go on a diet.

Grandma's arms were the world's best argument against diets. One arm around your shoulder could scatter the worst fears. Two together could hug away tears. They could say, "I'm so proud of you," "I love you," and "I'm happy to see you" all in one great yielding hug.

Grandma didn't talk much. She didn't have to. Somehow, she just *knew* what I needed or wanted. She always kept a candy bar in the refrigerator for my visits. We would wait together until my father (a dentist) and my mother (a believer in healthy snacks) said good-bye. Then she'd rush to the refrigerator for my delicious, secret treat.

These visits to Grandma's were always the same: a hug, a candy bar, a game of cards, a look at old pictures of her family back in Europe. So I was puzzled one day when Grandma forgot the cold candy bar.

Then Grandma began forgetting more than the candy. Her mind seemed elsewhere when we played cards. She made dumb mistakes. One day I heard her yelling at my grandfather for eating a sandwich she'd made for herself. But he hadn't eaten it. She had moved it from the kitchen to the dining room table and forgot. This scared me. I didn't understand what could be happening to my grandmother.

The first symptoms of Alzheimer's may not be detected by the patient's family. The symptoms might be as simple as not remembering the name of a person in a photograph.

DAYS OF FORGETTING AND CONFUSION

I didn't understand because at first no one knew that my grandmother had Alzheimer's disease. We didn't know that her forgetting how to play gin rummy was an early warning of more forgetting, more change, to come.

Alzheimer's is a *progressive* disease. That means it starts out mild and gets worse and worse. It is also a *chronic* disease. When you get the flu or the chicken pox, you get better after a week or two. The disease goes away. Not Alzheimer's. It doesn't go away by itself. And doctors don't yet know how to cure it.

The disease follows a nonstop course from forgetting to dementia. First, forgetting brings confusion. Confusion affects judgment. Patients can no longer work, handle money, or drive well. Their social skills begin to fall apart. An accountant cannot balance his own checkbook. A retired doctor goes out to buy the Sunday paper and gets lost on her way home. A woman drives through a stop sign, then yells at the driver whose car she almost hit. She doesn't know what she has done. A lifelong football fan goes to his friend's yearly Super Bowl party. He cannot follow the game. He can't understand what his friends are saying about it.

Over time, these problems get worse. Mood and personality change, too. Some of these changes are a result of

One symptom of Alzheimer's is not being able to remember a familiar route to one's home.

how the disease affects the brain. Some are a response to failing memory. Imagine going for a walk you have taken many times before. But this time, you don't know which way to turn to get back home. How would you feel? Upset? Angry? Scared?

Alzheimer's patients often deny they have a problem. But they have to find *some* way to explain the mistakes they make. They have to make sense of a world that no longer makes sense to them. My grandmother once accused a neighbor of stealing the sweaters she had misplaced. She started putting chairs in front of her apartment door to keep my grandfather from seeing another woman at night. There was no other woman, of course. My grandfather sometimes read while my grandmother slept. She forgot that. So, when she awoke once and he was not in bed, she decided he must be with somebody else.

SOMETHING'S WRONG WITH GRANDMA

The day my grandmother blocked the door with chairs, my grandfather called my mother. I heard her talking to him:

"No, Daddy, I don't know what's wrong. The other day she told me she needed to go shopping, but when we got to the store she couldn't remember what she wanted. Maybe

I should take her shopping every week. We can make a list together before we go…."

"I don't know. I don't know if this will pass. You know, she didn't recognize Sally the other day, and she's known her forever. When I said, 'Mom, it's Sally!' she said, 'Well, how could I recognize her? She dyed her hair.' Can you imagine? Sally's hair has looked the same for years!"

"…I'm worried, too, Daddy. Maybe she should see a doctor. Maybe she's going crazy."

Crazy? I heard that word and I wanted to scream at my mother, "You're the crazy one! Nothing's wrong with Grandma!" But I knew that wasn't true. Every time my parents took me to see her now, my mother and father stayed. And my mother made the lunch, always with enough leftovers to last part of the week.

I never tried to play cards with Grandma anymore. She said she wasn't interested, but I knew she really couldn't play. But we still looked at pictures. She remembered the old faces and the old stories. She'd put her arm around my shoulder and tell me the old favorite tales. I loved these moments. They made me believe Grandma was really still the same – until one day one of the faces was scratched out of a picture. Grandma got very upset when she came to that picture. She started muttering in a language I didn't understand. She shut the album angrily and walked away, still talking to herself in that foreign tongue.

Later, I asked my mother about the picture. She said something was wrong with Grandma. She told me we were going to take Grandma to a doctor who could figure out what was wrong. She told me the woman in the picture was an old friend of Grandma and Grandpa's. Grandma had scratched out her face because she thought Grandpa loved that woman, not her.

THE DISAPPEARING SELF

These painful events are typical of the suspicion and *paranoia* that often come with Alzheimer's disease. But even they are not the worst part of the disease. As the disease progresses, its victims have trouble making decisions. They forget the right order for doing things. Simple acts such as getting dressed, bathing, or eating become hard.

These familiar activities become hard for another reason, too. Alzheimer's disease affects movement. A patient may refuse food in part because he can't always get the spoon in his mouth. Another person may refuse to bathe because she fears falling.

At the same time, patients forget *why* things like bathing are important. In fact, they remember very little by this stage. Perhaps they know their names and the names of those who are closest to them. They may recall bits and pieces of the past. But they cannot learn anything new. They cannot remember what happened yesterday. Or this morning. Or an hour ago.

Many times, Alzheimer's affects movement; a patient may need more help going up or down stairs.

Alzheimer's disease is like an eraser that slowly but surely rubs out a person's self. In the final stages of the disease, patients are no longer aware of the world around them. They cannot talk. They cannot walk. They can no longer feed themselves or control their bowels. They are like infants once again.

WHY?

No one knows what causes Alzheimer's disease. Scientists know a lot about what happens to the brain once someone has the disease, however. They know, for example, that Alzheimer's kills brain cells in the parts of the brain most involved with memory, thought, and emotion. They can describe many of the specific changes, like plaques and tangles, that happen in these parts of the brain.

With each new finding, scientists ask "Why?" Why does this change occur? What might cause it? What *theory* might explain it? Scientists are testing many answers to these questions. One is that Alzheimer's is inherited. Another is that a *slow virus* causes the disease. Yet another is that *toxins* are involved.

Some scientists think that two or more such things must be present to cause the disease. They say that studies of how the disease is inherited support this idea. Scientists know that Alzheimer's disease is inherited in certain families. They have even found a *genetic defect* linked to the disease in these families. But, not all family members with the genetic defect get sick.

To further complicate things, scientists have found more than one "Alzheimer's *gene.*" One gene seems involved in some families; another gene seems involved in others. This leads researchers to suggest that one gene alone may not trigger the disease. Perhaps two or more

Although scientists know what happens to the brain once someone has Alzheimer's, they do not know why some people develop the disease.

genes are involved. Or maybe the gene makes someone more likely to get the disease, but a virus or toxin or other outside agent sets it off. No one knows.

What's more, all the families—about 50—with a known genetic risk get the rare early form of the disease. Do older Alzheimer's victims also have a genetic risk? Again, no one knows. So scientists keep asking, "Why?"

A VISIT TO A SPECIALIST

For the family of someone with Alzheimer's disease, the question, Why? takes a different form. As the loved one's behavior gets stranger and more unmanageable, family members ask, "Why is my mother (or father, or sister) acting this way?" And they usually take their question—and their relative—to a doctor.

My mother took my grandmother to a *gerontologist,* a doctor who treats older people. He gave my grandmother a regular physical examination and a number of special tests. He took a blood sample. He asked questions about the date and the president, which many people with Alzheimer's disease cannot answer.

The gerontologist asked my mother questions, too. He wanted to know about my grandmother's current health and past diseases. He asked about any medications she was taking. He asked if anything had happened recently, like a death in the family, that might have made her depressed. And he asked a lot about her strange behavior:

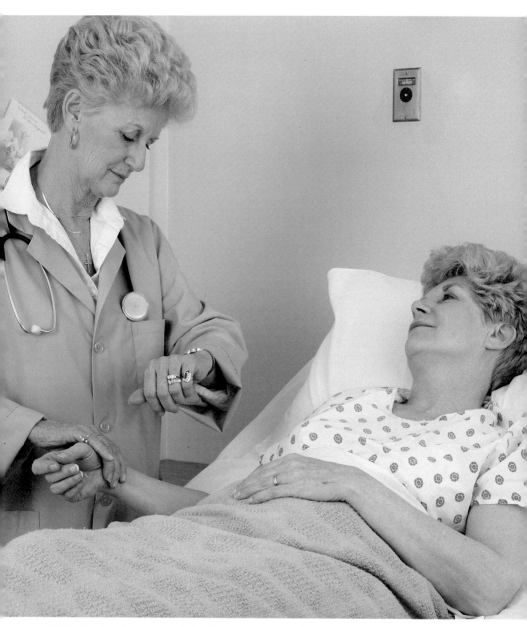

This doctor is a gerontologist, someone who specializes in treating elderly patients.

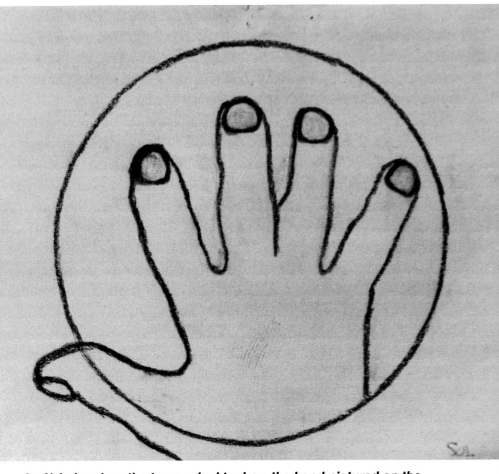

An Alzheimer's patient was asked to draw the hand pictured on the left. The patient drew the picture on the right, which is much smaller and has the wrong number of fingers.

28

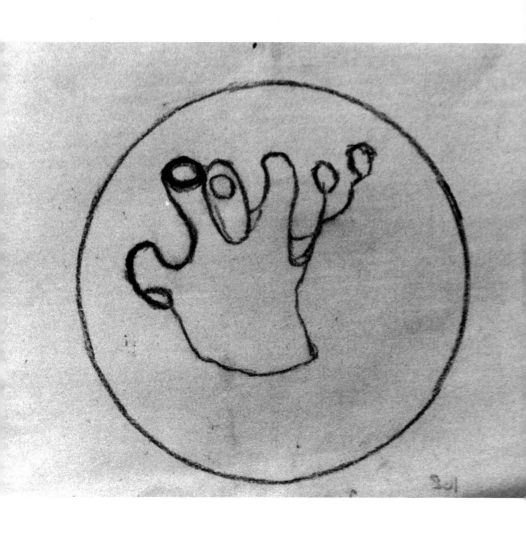

29

When had we first noticed it? What, exactly, did she do? Did the changes come all at once or slowly over time? How long did they take to become obvious? Did my grandmother seem to be getting worse or staying the same? He also asked that we take my grandmother for two more tests: an *EEG* and a *CAT scan.* An EEG shows electrical activity in the brain. A CAT scan takes X rays of the brain.

Finally, the gerontologist told my mother what he thought might be wrong. He said that my grandmother might have Alzheimer's disease. But he also said that he couldn't be sure. He explained that no blood test or X ray could detect Alzheimer's. The only way to tell if someone had it was to rule out other possible causes. That's why he wanted the EEG and the CAT scan. They could pick up problems such as a brain tumor or a stroke.

In the end, my grandmother's diagnosis remained "probable" Alzheimer's disease—probable because only an autopsy or brain *biopsy* could identify the disease for sure.

WHAT YOU CAN DO

Few illnesses bring as much pain to a patient's family and friends as Alzheimer's. This is because day in and day out, they watch someone they love fade away. No longer can they chat or joke, play checkers or watch television together. The person they love is no longer capable of these simple pleasures.

With each day, an Alzheimer's patient loses more of his or her memory and personality.

At the same time, family members must do more and more of what the person once did for him- or herself. They cook for, feed, dress, and bathe their loved one.

The family faces all the difficult questions that come with caring for someone whose mind is slipping away. How can we keep him safe? How can we help him continue to do as much as he can for himself for as long as he can? How can we let him know that we still love him? That we are still there to support him? And hardest of all, how long *can* we care for him? Will we reach a point when his needs are so great that we cannot meet them ourselves?

Specialists say family members can do a lot to help their relatives stay as safe and independent as possible. This is especially true during the early stages of the disease. Among their suggestions:

- Provide calendars and other reminders to help the Alzheimer's patient keep track of the time and day.
- Keep decisions simple. Let the loved one choose between two shirts to wear, not a whole closetful.
- Keep furniture and other things that are not dangerous where they have always been. Changes in familiar patterns can break the thinning threads of memory.
- Make the house safe, much as you would for a baby. Lock cleansers and other poisons away. Put tamperproof knobs on gas stoves. Keep knives out of reach. Lock doors so the Alzheimer's patient cannot wander off by him- or herself.
- Encourage the Alzheimer's patient to continue doing as much as possible for him- or herself.

Family members often wonder what is the best treatment for a Alzheimer's patient.

Nursing homes provide round-the-clock care for Alzheimer's patients. Here, a woman prepares to move into a nursing home.

Even though I was young, I know that I helped my grandmother. As long as she was able, I looked at her old pictures with her. This was part of our familiar routine. And for a long time, she still remembered some of the stories. Sometimes I read to her, although I don't know how much she understood. Sometimes I just sat and held her hand.

34

One daughter of an Alzheimer's patient said, "It's as if they have windows in their brains that open and shut." When the windows are open, the Alzheimer's patient's eyes might light with recognition. She may talk, ask to hear a record, ask who was just on the phone. But when they are shut, she is closed to the world. No one knows what she hears or sees or feels.

Most Alzheimer's patients reach a point when the windows are more often shut than open. Often, they need round-the-clock care. And family members need a rest from the fatigue and pain of caring for their loved one. Sometimes they can hire someone to help at home. Sometimes they must put their loved one in a nursing home. Hard as this decision was, that is what my family had to do with my grandmother.

A LAST VISIT WITH GRANDMA

The last time I saw my grandmother she sat in a hospital wheelchair, staring straight ahead, not talking. Her hair had gone from gray to white, its waves turned straight. She wore a short-sleeved hospital gown that rode too high on her legs, showing the skin hanging loose on her thighs.

Her skin hung everywhere – from her cheeks, her neck, even from the arms that once wrapped me in ample warmth. I could not bear to look at her. And so I stood behind her. I stroked her hair. I cried, knowing she could not see my tears.

She did not speak. I did not know whether she knew who I was. I did not even know whether she knew I was there.

When it was time to go, I kissed her cheek. I held her hand, hoping she could feel the love in my grip. "I love you, Grandma," I said.

She turned her head to me for the first time that afternoon. I saw the window open, the flash of recognition in her eyes.

"I love you, too, darling."

My grandmother, Ida Indik, died a month after I last saw her. She was bedridden and had stopped eating. Yet the night before her death, the window in her brain briefly opened. She asked for a dish of vanilla ice cream, her favorite, ate it, and closed her eyes. She died the following afternoon.

IS THERE HOPE?

Alzheimer's is a terrible disease. And it is touching more and more lives. The number of older Americans is growing at a faster rate than any other age group. As more people live longer, more get Alzheimer's disease.

But this increasing number of patients has a positive side. It draws more attention to the need for answers about

Doctors are not sure exactly what an Alzheimer's patient feels or thinks.

Alzheimer's disease. What causes it? How can we treat it? How can we cure it?

Five agencies of the federal government now support Alzheimer's research. One, the National Institute on Aging, funds 12 Alzheimer's disease research centers

Someday, researchers may find a cure for Alzheimer's. Until they do, older people and their families will continue to fear the disease.

around the country. The Institute says this program "is designed to speed us toward an understanding of what causes the disease and what can be done to treat it."

This research effort and others are helping. Although scientists do not yet know what causes the disease or how

to cure it, they do understand it better. And they have some promising leads on treatments.

For instance, scientists now know that Alzheimer's patients have too little of a brain chemical called *acetylcholine* (ə-set-l-'kō-lēn). They also know this chemical is involved in memory. So they are studying drugs that boost the amount of acetylcholine in the brain. One, called *THA*, shows promise for slowing memory loss. But so far, too few studies have been done to tell for sure. More are under way.

Scientists also know that blood flow to the brain drops in Alzheimer's patients. So they are testing drugs that reverse this. Like THA, some of these hold hope. But we still need to know many things: Which patients benefit? How much? From what amounts of which drugs or combinations of drugs? Do the drugs have *side effects?* If so, are the side effects so bad that people shouldn't take the drugs? Or are the drugs so helpful that people can put up with the side effects? As you might imagine, finding answers to these questions takes time – lots of time and many studies.

Other research may lead to the first definitive test for Alzheimer's disease. A chemical found only in Alzheimer's patients shows up in their *spinal fluid*. Peter Davies, the scientist who discovered this, says the chemical seems to be an early sign of the disease. Since doctors can take samples of patients' spinal fluid, they can test for the chemical – and the disease. A test to let them do this should be available soon.

In another study, scientist Barbara Talamo found that tissue high in the noses of Alzheimer's patients shows changes like those in the brain. If these changes happen *only* in Alzheimer's, they could provide a test for the disease. This is because the tissue can be biopsied. A doctor can take a small piece and study it under a microscope. Since Alzheimer's patients lose their sense of smell early in the disease, Dr. Talamo's research might lead to early diagnosis, too.

These findings are exciting because early diagnosis could lead to early treatment. And drug studies show that the earlier treatment begins, the better. The new drugs help people in the early stages of Alzheimer's the most.

What's more, Drs. Davies and Talamo's findings may lead to better understanding of the disease. They would allow researchers to study cell and chemical changes as the disease progresses in living patients. This has never been possible before.

Do we know what causes Alzheimer's disease? No. Do we have a cure? No. Is there hope? Most certainly yes.

A FINAL WORD

Some months before my grandmother died, I called her to say hello. She did not recognize my voice. She kept calling my mother's name, and I kept saying, "Grandma, it's me. It's Laurie, your granddaughter. It's me."

Not all older people get Alzheimer's; many live long and fulfilled lives.

She did not understand my words. After a few minutes, she put the phone down and walked away. She didn't hang up–she just walked away. I hung on. I thought she would come back. But she didn't. After five minutes of calling, "Grandma, come back. Pick up the phone. Grandma, it's me!" I hung up.

I went to my room and cried with rage. How could this happen? How could my grandmother not know me? As my rage and hurt and confusion died down, another emotion took their place: fear. I had an image of my grandmother as she put down that phone. In my mind, she looked wild-eyed and distant. And I thought: Is this all I will have left? When I think of my grandmother, will I always see her this way–her once gentle face tense with mistrust and panic?

That phone call happened many years ago; my grandmother has been dead a long time. And so, I have an answer to my question, Is this all I will remember?

The answer is no. I remember that phone call very clearly. I remember what my grandmother looked like at the end of her life. But I also remember the grandmother of cold candy bars and card games.

Alzheimer's disease stripped my grandmother of her ability to care for herself. It left her unable to say, "How are you, darling?" or to comfort me with a hug. But it did not take away my ability to care for her. It did not destroy my memory of soft comfort on Saturday afternoons.

Watching Alzheimer's slow, steady assault on someone you love is painful and exhausting. People who care for

Alzheimer's patients need time to heal, to rest, to grieve. But in the end, the memory of a shared lifetime, not just the memory of disease, is what is left. And those memories, for many of us, are sweet.

FOR MORE INFORMATION

For more information on Alzheimer's disease, write to:

National Institute on Aging
Federal Building, Room 6C12
9000 Rockville Pike
Bethesda, MD 20892

National Institute of Mental Health
5600 Fishers Lane
Rockville, MD 20857

Alzheimer's Association
70 East Lake Street
Chicago, IL 60601
800-621-0379

GLOSSARY/INDEX

ACETYLCHOLINE–*A chemical released at nerve endings and involved in memory.* 40

ALZHEIMER'S DISEASE–*A chronic, progressive brain disease that destroys the ability to think, feel, remember, and care for oneself.* 5, 6, 7, 9, 11, 12, 13, 14, 15, 19, 22, 23, 25, 26, 30, 36, 38, 40, 41, 44

AUTOPSY–*An examination of a body performed after death.* 7, 30

BIOPSY–*A study or examination of tissue removed from the body.* 30, 41

CAT SCAN–*Special X rays of the brain.* 30

CEREBRAL ARTERIOSCLEROSIS–*Hardening of the arteries in the head; a form of dementia.* 6

CHRONIC–*On-going.* 19

DEMENTIA–*A loss of mental ability; a failure of the brain to store and process information normally.* 7, 11, 12, 19

DEPRESSION–*A mental disease that affects mood and can have symptoms like those that accompany Alzheimer's disease.* 11, 13, 26

EEG–*A recording of electrical activity in the brain.* 30

GENE–*Material in the body that is inherited and determines the traits a person exhibits.* 25, 26

GENETIC DEFECT–*An abnormal gene.* 25

GERONTOLOGIST–*A doctor who treats older people.* 26, 30

GLOSSARY/INDEX

INHERITED–*Passed from one generation to the next through genes.* 14, 25

LIFE EXPECTANCY–*The number of years someone is expected to live.* 6

MENTAL DECLINE–*Loss of memory, intellect, judgment, and other thinking skills.* 5

NERVE CELLS–*Special cells that carry information in the brain.* 7

NEUROLOGIST–*A doctor who studies the central nervous system, which includes the brain.* 7

PARANOIA–*Unfounded fear and suspicion.* 22

PLAQUES–*Groups of dead nerve cell endings found in the brains of Alzheimer's patients.* 7, 25

PNEUMONIA–*A lung disease that is often fatal in the elderly.* 6

PRESENILE DEMENTIA–*Loss of mental ability that starts before age 65.* 9

PROGRESSIVE–*Advancing; getting more and more severe.* 19

SENILE DEMENTIA–*Loss of mental ability that starts after age 65.* 9

SIDE EFFECTS–*Unwanted, often harmful, effects of drugs.* 40

SLOW VIRUS–*A virus that takes many years to cause a disease.* 25

SPINAL FLUID–*The fluid around the spinal cord.* 40

GLOSSARY/INDEX

STROKE–*A sudden blocking of blood flow to the brain, which causes brain damage.* 6, 11

SYMPTOMS–*Outward signs of a disease.* 9, 11

TANGLES–*Hairlike nerve cell fibers that are twisted and tangled together in the brains of Alzheimer's patients; these fibers are straight in normal brains.* 7, 25

THA–*A new drug that shows promise for slowing memory loss in Alzheimer's patients.* 40

THEORY–*An unproven but well-supported idea about why something happens.* 25

TOXINS–*Harmful substances; poisons.* 25, 26